The Ghost Trio

Cover art by alamy.com

Interior typefaces: Garamond Premier Pro and Kepler Std.
Cover typefaces: Avenir and Copperplate

Cover design by Laura Joakimson
Interior design by Laura Joakimson

Library of Congress Cataloging-in-Publication Data

Names: Derrick, Clyde, author.
Title: The ghost trio / Clyde Derrick.
Description: Oakland, California : Omnidawn Publishing, [2022] | Summary: "The great love of your life is dead. But that doesn't stop him from communicating with you-or luring you to join him in the afterlife. To remain safely in this world, you accept the help of a professional medium who develops his own emotional agenda. The Ghost Trio takes us to the Prague of the past, where a love triangle like no other finds its chilling and unexpected resolution. Inspired by the ghost stories of such practitioners as Henry James and Daphne du Maurier, Clyde Derrick creates three vividly original characters whose passions defy both time and the accepted boundaries between the dead and the living"-- Provided by publisher.

Identifiers: LCCN 2022036292 | ISBN 9781632431127 (trade paperback)
Classification: LCC PS3604.E7548 G56 2022 | DDC 813/.6--dc23
LC record available at https://lccn.loc.gov/2022036292

Published by Omnidawn Publishing, Oakland, California
www.omnidawn.com
10 9 8 7 6 5 4 3 2 1
ISBN: 978-1-63243-112-7

The Ghost Trio

Clyde Derrick

OMNIDAWN PUBLISHING
OAKLAND, CALIFORNIA
2022

I think that house across the street is haunted, Mike said one night. We were both lying on the couch, heads at opposite ends, his white socks close to my face, trying to distract me.

The house with the music? I said, trying to concentrate on one of Henry James's lesser known ghost stories.

The house with the music that plays all night and the yard work that gets done even though we never see anybody, Mike said, looking at me through a rolled-up sports page.

I knew the house he meant. One house down and across the street from us, neither regentrified nor derelict, but teetering in between. There was something about that house, and that house only, a feeling as if something unique, even a little fearsome was coiled there. Vanilla light seeped out through the third story shutters on Saturday nights, and the erratic strains of Dowland, Beethoven and pre-fusion jazz often met my ears when I walked the dogs. I remember especially the unmistakable second movement of Beethoven's 'Ghost Trio' which I had just been savoring.

The front yard seemed to be managed by elves, for I would come out at six in the morning or half past eleven at night to find pots of flowers refreshed, the bougainvillea disciplined, the lawn fragrant with manure and reseeded, yet we never saw anyone diligently on their knees, grunting with a spade, at any time. Mike had every reason to suspect the house was haunted, and the night he made his observation, we also made a bargain that the first person who saw a human presence in that house would get the Sunday New York Times crossword exclusively for a month.

No sightings occurred for nearly two weeks. Trying not to look like the voyeur that I was, I kept checking the suspicious house while enjoying the harmless one we lived in. Childhood friends who had improbably come together later in life, Mike and I had been partners for nearly a year, and I had gratefully fled Los Angeles for Monterey to live with him. We had settled into a neighborhood mixing future and past, hope and forgetfulness in its houses, some blinking at the world again under glossy coats of new color and others wheezy and congested, their boards exposed and gray. Our house was close enough to the ocean for us to continually hear and smell and taste it. This was magically invigorating after thirty years of measuring each breath and neighborly breach in Los Angeles.

In this new life, we both made a practical point of avoiding people. I had had an unreasonable social life in Los Angeles and merely wanted to enjoy my new relationship. I had the solitude that the normal working day of a writer brought, fully supported by four dogs and two cats. Mike meanwhile had checked off two unhappy marriages and the relations that accompanied both; beyond me, his two adored daughters and a few friends from work who shared his noisy enthusiasm for sports, he wanted no other human presence in the house. So he was understandably surprised when I told him I wanted to invite the people in the haunted house over for dinner. I just have this feeling, I said. Mike half groaned, half hacked. My 'feelings' that promised us variety, intrigue or at least a good meal had sometimes led us to deserted or leveled destinations or literal dead-end streets, and were seldom very reliable.

I left a note at the door of the haunted house the following day, feeling a little silly at being both scared and excited. As I was leaving, I heard the door open and saw a woman pick up the note from the porch. Did you leave this? she asked.

I approached, finding her very likely in her late sixties, long cinnamon hair streaked with gray. She wore a sailor's sweater gone shapeless from overuse, equally shapeless slacks, and spotless new clogs. Her arresting gray eyes stared over reading glasses and the smell of something buttery and full of cardamom floated from the house in one warm breath. I remarked that Mike and I were fairly new on the street and wanted to get to know people here. She admitted that she and her husband avoided people like the plague, usually. I replied, So do we, usually.

That made us both laugh, and something in her body eased. My husband and I would be happy to come...any night is good for us. I'm Laurel and my husband's name is Alec, she added.

As I put together an ambitious meal four nights later, I felt a nut-sized pressure at the bottom of my stomach, a message that something unwelcome might come from this encounter. Mike arrived home from his work site hot, dusty and cranky: Do we have to do this? Laurel and Alec were late, which made Mike crankier, and as the couple entered the house, bringing singed irises from their garden and French bread dotted with fennel, I sensed that I was the only person who really wanted this social evening. The house was abnormally hot and no one was comfortable until I put on the Johnny Hartman and John Coltrane album that I had heard coming from Laurel and Alec's third floor window one night, which I knew Mike also liked.

Suddenly everyone smiled and relaxed. Laurel said in her oboe-like voice, We saw Johnny Hartman sing once in Chicago. Do you remember? Alec nodded, face expanding with a smile. Alec loves jazz, well, all kinds of music, Laurel murmured. Jazz in general went to jazz in Monterey to Mike telling them he owned a construction company here, then describing me as an interesting and not fully appreciated writer. Alec was a little older than Laurel and did not seem to match her at all. She was tall and serene, and I imagined intimidated the average suitor when she was young. He was short and kinetic, a Terrier with weedy white hair and the lost-in-my-head gaze of an obsessive academic. More like an older brother or professional colleague than Laurel's partner of forty or so years. Yet there were moments when they glanced at each other that made both Mike and me feel like intruders; naked looks of love not meant for a social gathering.

The talk throughout dinner was devoted to our experiences as transplants. Mike had been in Monterey sixteen years, I had been here one, and Laurel and Alec had moved here twenty years ago from Scotland, where he was born. They had met on holiday in the Czech Republic in the late Sixties when it was still Czechoslovakia, and settled in Edinburgh where Alec had been a professor.

Professor of...? Mike asked.

Alec was distracted by something and got up and looked out the window. Laurel looked after him, a little concerned.

Theology, Laurel said with strange discomfort. Religious

mystics, she added vaguely.

Something shifted in Alec, as if a new energy had entered his body. He snapped his head slightly and let himself seem distracted by our books.

Then it struck me. Wasn't Czechoslovakia closed off to Western countries in those years? I asked aloud.

Not with the proper academic credentials, Alec said dismissively. Laurel stopped short in what sounded like another reason altogether.

Mike looked at me with those blue flannel eyes and mouthed, Spies! while Alec and Laurel fished for cashews. I was thinking the same thing. Retired characters come out of the cold and John Le Carré, hiding with aliases in Monterey, California.

As if to distract us, Laurel added, I also taught at university. Twentieth century European music history. Something that's a bond for Alec and me, she said, and Alec nodded.

As I love what only serious music lovers will call 'serious music' and studied piano for years, I began to riddle them both with questions. Laurel and I were soon enmeshed in a discussion of the Eastern European composers we loved like Janáček and Martinů while I brought out an impatiently waiting dinner. For someone who was not a musicologist like Laurel, Alec certainly knew music and expressed his passions and dislikes, sometimes aggressively. Meanwhile, Mike was at sea but happy to focus on the flank steak, a bribe of sorts as I knew it was his favorite dish.

To be equitable I switched the topic to sports, where Laurel and I were out of our depth but Mike and Alec both displayed great passion. Laurel and I satirized them a bit, and soon we were all laughing as newfound Giants and A's fans. Mike joined me in the kitchen to dollop out dessert and murmured, They're cool. I'm glad we did this.

Not so cool, I felt, was the couple's intrusive lust which reappeared as I set dessert on the table.

My faultless flourless cake was upstaged by long looks and unfinished sentences. I had started to pour coffee when the couple ended their visit briskly, and Mike and I watched them nearly running back home together like two teenagers who have the house free for a few hours. Mike and I sat for a moment, slightly baffled in the wake of their visit.

Was it me saying that poppyseeds are an aphrodisiac? Mike said.

But seeing the older couple still so drawn to each other made us realize how long it had been since we were just as giddy, and it became an unexpectedly intimate night. Mike and I were both in unusually good moods for a week. Then we chanced upon more opportunities to get to know the couple: meeting Laurel and Alec while walking our dogs a few days later, then discovering them one Sunday afternoon in Pacific Grove, where we happily talked over each other and drank too much coffee.

Then we found more of their delicious bread on our porch along with a dinner invitation. Mike and I appeared early and found the front door wide open. We could hear the couple arguing and held back. What was most striking was that they argued in a language neither of us knew. But they certainly knew it and were anything but novice speakers.

Czech, Mike said. I've heard some of those words when

Novak gets pissed off.

Brian Novak was one of Mike's occasional crewmen and drinking buddies, whose grandparents had emigrated at the start of World War II. They're spies, Mike hissed. Cold war spies hiding in California.

Alec was recriminating, something I would never have predicted, his voice lower by an octave; an altogether different person from the man we had met in our own home. Then we caught a glimpse of them moving past the front window. Alec's body had taken on a ferocity it had never suggested before, and impatience swept his face in vivid strokes. Laurel also was a different person, defiant in a manner I can only describe as girlish, like an older actress mimicking a woman in her twenties.

I almost worried that they might come to a physical confrontation when, abruptly, a new feeling overpowered Alec that changed him—as if he knew they'd had this argument before and his fit of temper was unjustified. He dropped the china serving dish they were arguing about on the table and spun Laurel into the kitchen where they indulged in a more universal language. Mike and I wondered if we should come back after they had reconciled on the O'Keefe and Merritt. We started to leave when we heard clogs on the floor inside and turned to see Laurel emerging, flushed less from embarrassment than excitement at her own fiery spouse. Please forgive our silliness, she stammered, again like a much younger woman, and offered two glasses of a Spanish aperitif that was bitter but effective. Mike and I came in and sat at the dining table as she made excuses about finishing the meal, adding that Alec was lying down for a moment.

Fifteen minutes later Mike and I were about to suggest that we convene on another night when Alec stumbled out as if recovering from a seizure. His face was wet from the faucet, hair combed carelessly in all directions. Now then, he said, sitting down, how have you boys been?

The meal ranged from the exotic to the bungled as if the cook had been distracted, and Mike and I certainly knew just how. The mussels, clams and pasta in a piquant sauce extracted Czech exclamations, no doubt obscene, from Alec. Laurel blushed and kept rebuking him in a tender Czech. I just didn't know what to make of this little man: before, a modest and even pet-like professor of theology, and now, an earthy visitor from a former Communist satellite. He also kept staring at me, as did Laurel, in an uncomfortable way that literally made my head hurt. And yet, Mike and I were coming to love these people and their house with the sour milk walls that hadn't felt paint in years, the infestation of books in need of a dust cloth, the cats with spiked fur that passed with bored assessments of their guests. I realized that the majority of these books were music—some Baroque and classical, but mostly music of the nineteenth and twentieth centuries. Only then did my eyes find the hobbled baby grand in the corner, its varnish uneven and foggy, as well as a carefully positioned violin and clarinet, both looking well used and appreciated. My eyes met Alec's, who had been watching me take this all in.

You're a musician too? I asked.

Hobby, he said softly, looking down. Some hobby, I said, if you can play all this music and three instruments. Would you care to play now? I could take the piano part.

He smiled and shook his head. Soon perhaps, he said

warmly.

Mike and I settled into a sinking couch under dismal lights to sip the most electric coffee, and Laurel offered her intoxicating tart. We consumed it addictively and for an interval, no one knew what to say.

You know, we thought this house might be haunted, Mike blurted. I thought he might have said something more interesting until I saw Laurel was slightly ashen and Alec was unreadable.

What made you think that? Laurel asked.

Well Cluny and I, we grew up in a town full of haunted places. You might not think sunny, stupid Southern California would have any, but it does, Mike said. We've experienced some pretty weird things firsthand.

We've had our experiences, too, Alec said, taking Laurel's hand.

Please tell us about yours, Laurel prodded.

I don't know what possessed us, and I do use that word consciously, but Mike and I set off on a series of stories that took us into the late hours. The Vista Linda Methodist Church was the recurring setting for the best of the ghost lore of the town where he and I had grown up together. There was a notorious, long identified presence in the church's boiler room that purportedly was the spirit of a young man who had hanged himself there the night before Sunday services. Using a tattered book I'd found on setting spirits free, I had tried to free the man's spirit with high school friends one poorly planned night, with the only result that I had fainted from a noxious smell no one else detected. Visitors whether familiar or new to the church had also seen a man sitting in the wingback chair in the groom's room, wearing a suit from the Nineteen Teens, all dressed for a wedding but for his coat. Someone had connected him to a young man who had gotten cold feet and skipped his own wedding, but later recanted when his beloved married someone else. He had supposedly never married from heartbreak at his own false move, and people in town speculated that he inhabited that room as if waiting for a second opportunity to go to the altar.

One of our fourth grade classmates who had been killed by a reckless driver was known to be seen in a folding chair just outside the twelve card tables downstairs at Wednesday night bridge. You needed to be a newcomer to see her, and every newcomer described her perfectly, down to her Girl Scout uniform. The legendary Mexican American La Llorona, a footless woman sobbing for her dead children, swept not only through other cemeteries in the Southwest but through ours as well. She had been seen by school children out on a dare as well as two credible adults whose cars had either run out of gas or suffered a flat. We were tripping over each other excitedly telling these stories, and what fueled us were the beautiful faces of Laurel and Alec, who were utterly credulous and even moved. And then suddenly Alec fell back in his chair as if life had drained out of him, and Mike stopped mid-sentence.

Are you OK? Mike asked with alarm. Alec shook his head but not convincingly, and Laurel looked to us in such a way, we knew we had to leave quietly. Alec lay back in his chair looking to the ceiling, breathing unevenly. Laurel followed us and took both our hands at the door.

He's loved this, and he loves you both, she said. Laurel quietly closed the door on us and went to Alec with a concerned burst of Czech. Neither Mike nor I said the word 'spies' as we walked home slowly, looking back. We knew something had changed.

❧

The next morning, Mike and I left some oranges at their door with a note of thanks, and both of us had an uneasy day, sensing all was not right. Mike could not ignore an ambitious remodel he was overseeing, and unable to focus on a rewrite, I rode my bike for a few hours, always checking my phone. I returned home to find an ambulance backing out of Alec and Laurel's driveway, a stolid Laurel inside and staring down at Alec in the ambulance's gurney. She did not notice me as the vehicle lunged down the street and onto the main thoroughfare under a siren attack. I left a note for her, asking Laurel to let Mike and me know if she needed anything.

Mike had just come home with a patina of sawdust when he and I turned to see Laurel in our door. Together we hugged a limp, surrendering woman who before had only shown physical reserve. Heart problems, she said before we could ask. Nothing is blocked, but it's just that the old ticker is just that—old. He asked me to go home and so did the hospital staff.

Mike settled Laurel into a dining chair and reassured her till we could throw a slapdash sandwich before her, but she simply studied the blank tablecloth. You know, I've grown so fond of that little man, she said quietly. Mike and I looked at each other; it wasn't exactly what we expected a passionate woman in a forty-year relationship to say of her beloved.

She read our reactions correctly, and smiled. So, my dear new friends, she said, I should tell you a ghost story of my own. Or our own. Alec's and mine...and a certain other spirit's.

❧

I had the most typically normal life a girl could have in the Nineteen Fifties and Sixties, growing up in the most placid town in America with the dearest and most benign family. Safe, safe,

safe—most of the time, but not all, as you shall hear. My father worked for a medical supplies distributor and the family lived well in a conscientious little town outside Seattle that no one can afford anymore. I had two sisters and a brother, all lovely, compliant, sensible people, barring that rebellious period we all know from thirteen to nineteen years old. And then safe, safe, safe when it came to their college, career and marriage choices.

Only I was not part of this pattern. I overheard my mother and father talking one day when I was eight years old, in the third grade. They thought no one could hear them, and my father expressed the concern that 'Laurel seems detached.' My mother said with an ice cube in her voice that, 'The girl seems...' And then she jumped into the word: 'haunted.' That made me smile and feel special, which I don't think was their intention. And looking back, I was, absolutely, haunted. It always felt to me, even as a young child, that my life at that time was not the beginning of something new that everyone thought it was. I knew that something else had come before, and at some point, I would return to that something else, whatever it had been, if only to visit.

We weren't a religious family, but like most such families, we turned to the nearest available minister in a crisis when our inner resources failed us and we had no quick answers. I'd seen the inside of the Lutheran church for only a few baptisms, including my own, but I knew Pastor Litka from his own children at school and felt very much at ease with him. My mother brought me to see him one day after school and he offered me a few cookies on a lamb-shaped plate and a glass of milk. It was just Pastor Litka and me and the stale air of his office. We talked about school and hobbies and whether or not I trusted the Lord Jesus Christ. I figured the answer to that had to be 'yes' to avoid a lecture.

At some point I saw that the red-headed man was sitting in the room, not with us exactly, but in a wingback chair to the side. I had seen him a number of times before. Once when my parents were having a barbecue he had come through the back gate and blended easily into the gathering. No one said hello or noticed him, but he came to where I was swinging on the swing set, and pushed me in the swing—very hard and far too high. My mother shrieked and one of the men quickly placed himself to catch me when the swing swooped back. I was giggling about my moment of danger and how it stopped the party, even though it scared me as well. When my mother came to scold me at how high I had gone, I told her that the red-headed man had given me an extra hard push. But there was no red-headed man anywhere to be seen. The guests looked among themselves and laughed at the impossibility of a crop of red hair among us.

I didn't laugh, because I knew more than they did. I had also seen the red-headed man when I was alone in an aisle in the supermarket. He appeared to be studying the different cereals, and then looked at me very meaningfully and tipped his hat. My mother called me and again, he was gone. I also saw him twice walking home when I had stayed after school for piano lessons and no one was on the street going home except him and me. He always kept a distance and then would turn or disappear when an adult came along.

The red-headed man was a nice-looking man, always in a black suit that seemed to be a little small and uncomfortable, a white shirt with a collar that was confining, and a black hat. I assumed that he lived somewhere in town and was harmless and our meetings were accidental. But now that he was here in the office with the minister and me, I thought that perhaps he was Pastor Litka's friend or worked for the church. Of course! That explained his suit. Maybe he was a religious man too.

Your mother tells me that you have a special friend, Pastor Litka said without looking at me directly. I knew that adults only looked away when something made them uneasy. I thought he meant my friend Julie Fletcher and started to describe her, but Pastor Litka interrupted me. No, Laurel, I mean the red-headed man. Isn't there a red-headed man that you consider a friend?

I looked to the red-headed man sitting just behind the pastor. He smiled and put his finger to his lips, as if to say, this is our secret. I remember working my lower lip with my teeth, trying to figure out what to say next. I sensed that if I told Pastor Litka about the red-headed man, I would be in some kind of trouble, and I could hear my mother being hysterical as she was sometimes about things that didn't matter. So I told the pastor that the red-headed man was an imaginary friend.

Pastor Litka really was a kind man. He wasn't looking to shame anyone and understood children, having four of his own. He smiled and asked me to tell him about my imaginary friend. I made up a few wonderful characteristics to portray the red-headed man as a protector, looking out for me when I was alone. I wanted my mother to feel that I was safe and being watched out for. The pastor nodded and in five minutes, he believed he had convinced me to look to Jesus Christ for protection instead. I went along with that, all the time remembering my father talking about religion as 'hogwash' on bright Sunday mornings.

My mother was light and cheerful that night spooning out her gluey tuna noodle and frozen pea casserole, and I figured that the pastor had reassured her that there was nothing exceptional about me. Meanwhile I had learned that the red-headed man was my special secret not to share with anyone or I'd have to spend an hour with Pastor Litka again, when I would rather be home reading Nancy Drew. The red-headed man visited me several times a year up through high school. Once it was while I was getting into my clothes for school, about seventeen, and I turned and found him sitting at my desk, and his eyes went up and down my body. I cried out in alarm and he turned to nothing, like he'd stepped into a narrow slit in reality.

I'd overheard girls talking in the locker room, saying that being Catholic was more powerful than being Protestant because you could call on a saint or the Virgin Mary to protect you. (When the Protestants protested that they could call on God or Jesus, the Catholic girls cried out, And how busy are *they?*) I knew there was a convent in town and it had a gift shop with all kinds of religious paraphernalia. I mentioned to the nun behind the cash register that I had a friend who was Catholic who believed that she was being watched by an evil spirit. The nun clearly relished this sort of conversation and took twenty minutes to make several recommendations, embellishing the colorful histories of the saints. I put the St. Benedict medal on once the church was out of sight and did not see the red-headed man again until I was twenty-two years old, and supposedly on my way to Spain and, uncharacteristically, had forgotten the medal in my haste.

So let's jump to the close of college and my degree in the mostly wonderful if impractical field of musicology, which simply rattled my parents. Though I was an indifferent musician at best, I was an ardent and adventurous listener. I'd come to love the history of music, the stories of the composers, and finally, analyzing their work. My favorite music was that of the Czech composers leading up to World War II—Smetana, Dvořák, Suk, Janáček, Martinů. That mesh of the European with the Eastern and Asiatic, nothing made me quite as excited. I would have done anything to go to Prague, the center of

Czech music, but with Czechoslovakia then a Communist country, it was impossible for me to go there as an American. It seemed a shame as well because I attended a huge state university where I'd had the opportunity to study the Czech language with four other eccentric students. Spain (and its music) were second on my list, and much to the displeasure of my parents, I had saved for and booked a trip to celebrate my own graduation and informed them the day before departure. (I had not changed since childhood.) They were frantic and uncharacteristically loud.

I had paid for my round trip tickets and booked my hotels in advance of course, intending to make a slow path through Seville, Cordoba, Madrid, and Barcelona. But when I arrived at the airport, I was told that my flight had been cancelled due to worker strikes in Spain, and no flights would head there for days. The airline was rerouting its customers and even paying for train fare and hotels in other countries to keep them happy. I was practically pushed onto a flight to Vienna with assurance that my train trip from Vienna to Spain would more than compensate for the inconvenience.

I didn't even have a moment to notify my family—the flight was boarding momentarily. Flying over Spain to Vienna, I tried to focus on how this would work out rather than the unavoidable feeling that some force was behind this last-minute re-routing. I was delivered to the Wien Westbahnhof, and confused as to which train to board, I made a path to a sleeper car I was absolutely sure was headed to Paris. I fell like a stone into the long padded seat that would have folded out had I enough energy to do so. I vaguely remembered coming out of my sleep to wave my passport at a man in a blue cap.

Not many hours later I heard someone announce *Praha*, and I sat up to find it was afternoon and I was not in Strasbourg or Paris as I had expected, but in Prague. The people around me were speaking a language I knew well enough—Czech. I also knew that this country was Communist—it was 1967—and my being here as an American was, well! Certainly problematic, and very likely not tolerated.

I was virtually ignored by customs officials more interested in the Russian and Bulgarian tourists and their Party connections. My Czech made it impossible for me to arouse much suspicion, and my *kroners* could be translated to Czech *koruny*, and were before I got very far within the *Praha hlavní nádraží*. This train terminal I suddenly recalled with nostalgia, as if it had been the platform for trips in the past.

I was not even out of the train station when I bought myself a *trdelník*, thinking involuntarily that it had been such a long time since I had indulged in the sugary pastry and missed the aroma of them cooking in the little booths on the street. I knew my way to Wenceslas Square where patriotism for the Czech nation surged within me, and I decided that lunch at the Grand Hotel Europa was a necessity, as was another dessert. I then rushed to the Old Town Square and the Hus monument, thinking to myself that while an indifferent Protestant at best (even forgetting my medal of a Catholic saint), I had great respect for the Protestant martyr's courage. I delighted at finding the Astronomical Clock, which I had missed, and then remembered one of the lanes twisting off the square to a very small park where I thought I might like to read on one of the iron benches, with the company of a monument to the soldiers of the Great War. But also I wanted so dearly to cross the Charles Bridge and see Prague Castle. Saying hello to the Vltava, the river that runs through Prague, I virtually ran across the bridge toward the castle which regarded me as an old distant relative would, trying to remember whose child I was.

When I came upon the Church of St. Nicholas in Malá Strana,

I found myself amid a scattering of memories like hailstones on a windshield, so random and confusing that I had to go inside the church and settle into a pew. Feeling lightheaded from too many sweets and too little sleep, I said in Czech, 'How wonderful it is to be home.' I then decided that what I really meant was, how glad I was to be in a wondrous place I thought I could never in my life enter. I didn't miss Spain for even a flash.

The dimness of the church finally pushed me outside where I took in the castle from a bench, believing that I *remembered* a long-established beer garden near the castle and its snapping sausages. Seeking it out I saw more life on the streets than American TV news and Cold War movies would have led me to expect. There was music bursting from community halls and cellar clubs, people my own age debating and laughing, their modish oranges, pinks and turquoises flashing against the brown weariness of the buildings. I had no prescience that this cultural thaw would be trampled a year later by Soviet thugs in uniform, nor that the Czechs had only known such freedom in a handful of years between the First and Second World Wars.

And then I felt compelled to flag down a taxi and give directions in Czech to the driver to head out of the city to a place I thought I didn't know (and it would turn out, I actually knew quite well). The driver looked at me curiously and asked me when I was last in Prague. I can't remember, I said, and it felt like I was telling the truth.

I knew the drive that, in twenty minutes, led to the outskirts of the city, to the former estates that now housed multitudes of residents according to the Communist plan. I had to remind myself to breathe as the car turned left to scuttle down a dry rutted dirt path that turned into firmly set flagstones under interlacing trees. And then a sign made me gasp yet again: The Damek Svoboda House and Museum.

The driver asked me if I would like for him to wait. I surprised him by saying I wanted to walk back into the city. That's a long walk, dívka, he said in a voice as baggy as his eyes.

I stood with my duffel bag before a manor house from the eighteenth century, a residence of four stories on a small footprint where a prince had probably kept a mistress instead of a family. I couldn't fight the inclination to cry as I found my way to a stone bench just outside the door to the house. Crying from relief, from sadness—and I realized, from fear. It abated when I heard a single pianist at his instrument, somewhere in the house.

It was music I knew but couldn't identify, and I was drawn through a rotten wooden gate and untamed birches to the back of the house, where there was a nude, cleanly swept stone terrace. The French door to a room on the third floor was open and music came over the balcony like runaway smoke. The player repeatedly stopped at the dead end of a phrase, would return to where he'd started, play again, and stop again at the musical dead end.

I saw the doors on the ground floor were ajar and let myself into what had been a salon or drawing room of the house. I climbed the familiar stairs to the third floor, thinking, It is so difficult to keep up this house, thank goodness we have help. I heard a man's voice upstairs exclaim in irritation, *Hovno*, and I smiled recognizing the Czech word for 'shit.' I knew which room to enter, a room where the red-headed man of my childhood sat at the piano, robust, barrel shaped, a forgotten beard and eyes of gray slate, erasing what he had written on one of a score of messy sheets of composition paper. Coffee, please, he said to me.

Am I your servant now? I replied.

Today, yes, every day, yes! he said in anger. And then handsomely:

Listen to this, Anneliese.

Anneliese; the name made me list like a ship. He started to play the piece he'd been thwarted by since I arrived, a piece that fused the romantic with the modern. The way I heard it, these two strains almost talked to each other, and I thought he was a genius for doing it. I smiled and sat down. I saw I was no longer in my American capris, tennis shoes and a cotton sweater, but a formal dress with a sweater, both of dark blue wool, and rather ugly shoes of another time altogether.

Damek, the red-headed man, came to that impassable juncture and threw out another *Hovno!*

Stop forcing it, I said as if I knew him well. Take a walk, have an apple. Do something else anyway. You'll find your way on those keys when you come back.

He stopped suddenly and I could tell that whatever emotion he felt was difficult for him, and it had nothing to do with the ungrateful piece of music. Not looking at me, he murmured: You said you were not coming back.

This is my house too, I said, completely sure of what I was saying.

Always? he asked.

Always, I answered.

I am forgiven?

I am finding a way to forgive you, I said, not completely convinced.

He stopped working and looked at me with obvious want. At once I knew in one clap against my head that I had never loved anyone this deeply or well. I knew what it was like to listen to the music of the great Czech composers with him in a darkened hall and see the excitement in his eyes, to hear him talk about his aspirations and difficulties in creating music. To stare at him as he napped in an overstuffed chair, to carry his sobs at the death of his grandmother and exasperation at a spoiled piece of meat. I knew what it meant to couple with him, to be dominated and soothed by him. I knew what it was like to be with him in a bed for a full day and night and never sleep. He kept his eyes on me as he rose and crossed the room. I felt his body against mine, his arms and mouth forceful, then tender, then forceful again. I heard the lake lapping at the shore through the open door to the balcony, the children skirting its edge with laughter, water slapping boat hulls and timid oars. The red-headed man who I knew as Damek and I then held each other, and I could smell his male smell, like no one else's. I felt him guiding me to the open door and the balcony. Don't the sounds of the lake bring you peace, Anneliese? he whispered. You do love the lake so, Anneliese.

Then I was jarred to find another set of hands taking my shoulders from behind and the red- headed man folding up like a tablecloth. I looked down to see that I was pressed against a crumbling stone railing—sure to fall three stories to the stone terrace if I weren't held back.

The rescuing hands belonged to a friendly little Scotsman, and he backed me away from the edge of the balcony with his hands and spotty Czech. When I made out the Scottish accent, I responded in English, thanking him over and over. He turned me and got a good look at me, and registered the kind of surprise you see when someone thinks they recognize you.

Tell me...what made you walk to the edge of the landing there? he asked like a therapist.

Shaken as I was, I could tell harmless, adaptable Alec, anything, and did, the whole episode. He invited me downstairs to a kitchen that smelled of natural gas and beer and rifled through a cupboard to find, ironically, Spanish sherry, which made me smile. After I had a few jolts of the drink, he said, Are you familiar with Damek Svoboda?

Possibly, I said, thinking about the red-headed man.

Miss, this house was the residence of Damek Svoboda, one of this country's most gifted yet least known composers, and his wife, a woman named Anneliese Kammerer. Perhaps I might show you the rooms they lived in, and the little museum here that tells about their lives.

I followed Alec to a sitting room, and I remember there were some unexpected voices elsewhere in the house negotiating a charge for a plumbing repair. Alec promised to leave me only briefly. I was distracted by a painting on the wall that also had a familiar tug to it, and then I looked up to find I was no longer in a well-upholstered sitting room, but a very common kind of room, a kitchen. An old woman was setting out pastries and coffee on a shy little table. I thought I knew this woman too, and when she turned to show her plaited white hair, her scrubbed face and the gap between her two front teeth, I knew her at once as Damek's grandmother.

Please sit, Fräulein Kammerer, the woman said, and I took one of the roughhewn chairs at the table, noticing that I myself was wearing a light rose-colored jacket and white skirt, and that it was hot. There was activity outside the window that seemed impossible in a country house; people on foot and bicyclists passing.

I apologize for the simpleness of my home, but I can only offer you coffee here in the kitchen, the grandmother said. Růžina, I said to her; may I please call you that, and you may call me Anneliese? You needn't call me 'Fräulein Kammerer.'

Everyone in Prague knows the Kammerer Glass Factory, and your family, Růžina said somewhat resentfully, pouring coffee into cups faded by time and scrubbing. I knew the factory too, what it smelled like and how the workers with their gleaming warm faces would remove their hats to bow to me.

The fact that I come from a prosperous family does not mean I cannot care for your grandson, or you, I said. The pastry had studded her fingers with sugar like little jewels.

What have you learned about my grandson Damek? The woman Růžina was mournful in saying this. What do you truly know?

No family is perfect, I said, winning some respect when I declined the cream and sugar. I know that you took care of him when his mother could not.

And his father?

Damek never knew him, I replied lowly.

I raised him to be a good Catholic, and I wish he had kept with the organ and his church music, Růžina said, taking none of the coffee or pastry.

I don't think he has turned his back on church music, I responded. He has the potential to be a great composer, and many great composers have returned to music that is sacred. Mozart and Bach both did, and so has Janáĉek.

I became aware of a scraping sound, and some unnerving laughter just outside the door, a door that led to the back alley perhaps, and then a brazen rattle. Růžina's face hardened for a moment and I rose with difficulty. I can answer the door for you, I said.

It's not for you, Růžina said in such a startling way that I stayed back as the old woman went to open it. There was another woman waiting on the step, perhaps in her late thirties but seeming much older. A woman trying to hold tight to her beauty though her obvious self-abuse— drinking? drugs?—was quickly eroding it.

You have something for me? the wasting woman said, flinching, tugging at her collar, shifting her hat. A little too much powder.

Clothes that were second hand, out of fashion. A man behind her who looked no more reliable than she. Růžina went to the cupboard and removed a reticule, drawing *koruny* from it. The wasted woman glistened and ran her tongue along her upper lip, but Růžina held back from giving it to her. Tell me, Katica, where are you living now?

Katica, the wasted woman, drew herself up as if insulted. I am doing fine, *Matka*.

Where do you live? Is it with this man? Růžina said.

We live comfortably enough, Katica said, now give me the money you promised.

Růžina held the currency back as if Katica had one or two more tricks to perform. Nodding toward me, Růžina said calmly: This young lady is in love with your son, Katica. Can you tell her who Damek's father was?

Katica's look of hope went instantly to shame.

And will you tell Fräulein Kammerer that when you sold yourself, you sometimes also sold your son, for others to touch and mistreat? Růžina exploded: A child! Who you let be touched by filthy men—

Katica came at the woman and grabbed the bills from her, and then made for the door, turning just to glance at me, so weakly! I felt hot and swallowed hard. Katica tried a few words but gave them all up and swung noisily out of the house, hitting her companion to erase his startled expression; and they were gone. I stood with dignity as the old woman shut the door.

That was a poor trick on your part, I said.

The boy cannot really love you, Růžina said quietly, in the way that you want to be loved, and ought to be. He was ruined at a young age. He can trust no woman.

I believe he trusts me, I declared.

I cannot stop you from what you want to do. But there is only *hoře* ahead for you if you persist. The memories of his mother and what she did will always be lying with you both in bed. Forgive me, dear Lord, for uttering this shame.

Růžina crossed herself and turned her back to me, and the noises of the street, the smell of the kitchen, fell back like a wave. I found myself once again facing Alec, stunned by what he must have seen; certainly not Růžina or Katica, but me in another forced transfer to the past.

Shall we learn about Damek's history then? he said to me.

I just got one significant piece of it, I replied; and then told him what I had experienced. Alec fed me the missing details; that once Růžina realized that her own daughter had prostituted her grandson, she had funneled the bewildered child into a regimented life of Catholic devotion which he drank like warm milk, planning a life as a priest. One of the priests caught the boy at the organ when he thought no one was around, picking out hymns with an infallible ear. The priest convinced Damek to pursue musical study under the wing of the cathedral organist, for which the boy showed an astonishing aptitude. He became assistant organist at sixteen and at eighteen he was performing his own compositions at services and concerts. One of the score of local young women who developed an attraction for the handsome and pious young composer was Anneliese Kammerer of the wealthy glass-making family. With a trust available to her at the age of eighteen, she gave the twenty-three year old Damek Svoboda an opportunity to devote himself entirely to the composition of his own music.

I remember then asking Alec: Why are *you* here? A Scotsman in Prague?

Ostensibly, theological research, he replied. I'm an assistant professor in Edinburgh. But this work at present, well, it's not truly part of my scholarship. I connect with—

It's his ghost that lives here, isn't it? Damek's, I said, impatient with the man's Scottish civility. And he *wants* me here.

Yes, from these experiences you've had in such a short time, I believe you were Anneliese Kammerer, Alec said simply. In my work as a theologian, my focus has been the study of mystical texts in all religions, and this nonconformist path has led me to places like this, and spirits like Damek. But perhaps, not so destructive a spirit as Damek.

Not so destructive. That did not sit well.

Alec continued, It might seem like you are hallucinating, but this phenomenon which we call 'transmigration' has happened at many historical sites including Versailles and been documented many times as well. People literally find themselves walking in the past. Here or elsewhere, he will continue to draw you into recollections of the past as you experienced earlier today, and again and again your life will be in danger unless you work with me to release him. Damek was deeply in love with Anneliese and I suspect, from what happened on that terrace, he would like you to...like you to join him, and be with him in the afterlife.

Before you could say *Hovno*, I'd found my way out of the house and was walking back to Prague with my bag and a headache from the whole afternoon. But this journey was persistently thwarted: an overturned milk truck, East German tourists wanting directions, a detour sign that sent me far afield. It took me two hours to make a distance that should have taken half an hour. That enabled Alec to catch up with me and beg me to come back and at least hear him out.

He'd prepared a meal which I was very happy to eat while hearing his appeal. There is something I haven't explained to you, he said, or rather, you didn't give me time to explain. You noticed that you didn't get very far from the house that Damek and Anneliese lived in. I expect that your coming to Prague, especially as an American, might also have felt as if someone were pulling the strings.

I shared how I originally intended to go to Spain, and then shared the stories of the red-headed Damek visiting me as a girl. Alec's eyes glistened like those of a great scientist finding his breakthrough. I felt a more like a laboratory animal than I liked.

We can stop these visitations forever, he said. This is how we can release him, and you from his control. You will need to allow his spirit to engage with you in conversation and living memory—

with me carefully watching and protecting you—until you find you are amidst what would have been Anneliese's last moments with Damek.

And those were...? I am sure I did not at all sound pleased.

Alec took a ponderous breath (as he tends to do). The day she died, he murmured, they were in this very house that they shared, in the room where you met his ghost earlier. Their housekeeper reported an argument that led to Anneliese falling to the terrace outside where she died at once. No one knows for certain if her fall was accidental or if Damek provoked it. We can surmise that he was so distraught witnessing this and surely feeling responsible that he quickly followed her.

Followed her?

He jumped from the third floor to die beside her.

I was terrified, wondering why this was happening to me, and if I had to go through any kind of ritual at all. But in that wonderful way that he has, Alec reassured me: We will work together, you and I, to let Damek draw you back into this scene. What you will need to do is dissipate the fight, and however possible, show your love for Damek, then encourage him to move on to the next life. In short, you must give him the resolution he never had.

And what do you gain from all this? I asked him. The little man said with the dearest sincerity: I cannot adequately describe what it means to me to bring resolution to a soul in crisis. It is a calling far transcending theological study. I do acknowledge the danger of putting oneself at such risk. This Damek Svoboda has been very stubborn, and I prayed that whatever I might be lacking would be provided to me. Here, now, I am certain that missing element has arrived, and it is you, Laurel.

I asked him how it was that Damek Svoboda could haunt this house and yet find me on the other side of the world. Alec told me that concepts like distance and time are irrelevant on the spiritual plane. And when spirits are deeply connected...inconsequential.

I should say that by this point, it was clear that Alec was, well, infatuated with me, I think for several reasons. He was infatuated with me as Laurel Glessing, a bright, confident and not unattractive young woman; he was infatuated with me as Anneliese Kammerer, who also had a fair amount of desirability; and he was infatuated with me as the solution to a challenge that had seemed without any kind of resolution. I understood why he felt that way, or these ways

I should say. Meanwhile I thought he was a kind man, a sincere one, but I felt nothing more than that. I was not one of those people who has an ideal in mind or even a picture of what a loved one might be. I had had passing crushes but nothing that would constitute honest-to-goodness love. I had a suspicion that when I found it, romantic love that is, it would be profound. And it was— but not with Alec.

Back to that kitchen. There came a rustle at the door and an aged woman bent in cautiously. I wasn't sure if it was another spectral visitation until she and Alec exchanged greetings and I accepted her roughened hand. I learned later that she was merely in her early sixties, but the combination of relentless work, Communist hardship, and harsh cigarettes made her look a good ten years older. Dressed in a conventional shirt and blouse, like a teacher expecting her class, she had dashed her imposing cheeks with rouge, and over her blue marble eyes danced spiders of clotted mascara. Her silver and black hair was restrained in a careless bun that might topple at any moment. The woman suddenly looked at me with what only can be called recognition, brought a permanently bent hand to her lips, and with something like anguish, fled the room.

Then I understood and looked at Alec, who was nodding. She

knew Anneliese, I said.

And adored her. That was Duša, he explained, the housekeeper who's been with the house since she was a girl.

Alec led me into a formal room on the first floor which had been converted to the small museum he had mentioned earlier. The smoggy cases traced Damek's life from boyhood to his untimely death just after the Munich Pact in 1938...only thirty-eight years old. Alec took me to the two cases that traced Damek's personal relationships, especially with Anneliese Kammerer. I can't describe what it feels like to see photographs in a museum that seem as if they are your own, poking at your sense of recall. After a few minutes, you're convinced you remember everything you see in them. It is not as if Anneliese and I were identical, but we could be mistaken for each other in passing. Enough of a resemblance to make me leave the room and find my way to the garden.

There, shortly, I heard over my shoulder, a crackling voice saying in Czech: You are so much like her. I turned and the old woman suddenly embraced me, and I felt relieved by this, in part because that embrace, too, felt familiar. Alec offered later that because she had been with the family for many years, she remained with the house at the request of the Czechoslovakian government and received a small stipend to care for the house and answer any visitors' questions about Damek Svoboda.

Alec coaxed us back into the formal sitting room and brought us tea and *susenky* where we talked for, oh, it seemed hours. As Duša opened up with more and more animation about the family, I could see the young woman I had known in the 1930s emerging from the wrinkles and sunken planes of her face. It was Anneliese that Duša was forever indebted to, Anneliese who had been easygoing and friendly with the servants, who had elevated her in the ranks until she oversaw the staff. Duša had no special affection for Damek! In her opinion, he never fully appreciated Anneliese: he would ignore her to get lost in his music, or go out drinking, and was known for striking her a few times. When I heard this, I shuddered and believed her. The only thing about Damek that Duša respected was his music which she knew was important to the Czech people and could fill her with pride. But she also found it a little too 'modern' and preferred Smetana, if she had to choose.

I laugh now when I think of her saying to me, I do think you could have done better by marrying that nice German gentleman you knew, even if he *was* German.

The German gentleman? I echoed.

I do not remember his name, she said. You grew up together, your families had talked about your marriage. His family owned something like a paper factory—

Gunther, I said quickly, and I was not even noticing or caring that Duša had started addressing me as if I *were* Anneliese. And yet the memory of the German man would still not surface; but Alec marveled that I, Laurel Glessing that is, had pulled the right name out of the ether. And then Duša began to cry, holding my hand, and I moved across the couch and put my arm around the woman.

I could not quite understand what Duša was saying amid sobs, and Alec gently said, Duša found them...the bodies of Anneliese and Damek.

I felt something go through me like a rod of the coldest steel. And then I righted myself, as I saw now what Alec had described—that only I could complete that strange and unpleasant process. I remember holding Duša so tightly in my resolution that she cried out.

Alec delicately suggested that Duša and I stay together in the same room, as Damek might try to lure me away in my sleep and it was careless for me to sleep alone. I slept in Duša's room on a quite luxurious couch made up as a bed. I didn't wake up with any clear memories of my dreams, only vaguely knowing that I had seen and spoken with people from another time, and all of this was in Czech.

The following day, I remember Alec, to make a good impression, had changed his shirt and combed his hair, which was not his wont. The three of us sat in the house, or strolled, or chatted, and nothing happened. It was as if Damek had already left, and I suggested this hopefully, but both Alec and Duša shook their heads. Oh, he is here! Duša said with delightful mistrust. He likes to flick my ear with his finger, because if he tries anything else, any nasty surprises in the soup or in the silver drawer, I put out little dishes of spirits of ammonia, which he hates.

Alec went into the city to pick up some wine and staples and came back excitedly with news. That night at the Church of St. Nicholas where Damek had first touched the keys of an organ, there would be a concert of his organ and chamber music. Duša admitted she was not that excited by his music, and then jumped forward as if someone had flicked her ear; and then she spoke to the ghost of

Damek Svoboda with no humor or fondness at all.

We all dressed formally, Alec in a rumpled suit pulled from its grave in a suitcase. The sight of it made Duša utter an untranslatable declaration, and she pressed his suit with a clicking tongue before we left the house.

At the cathedral, I automatically walked through an impassable crowd to a pew which was occupied and heard myself saying in Czech that this was my family's pew. The people sitting there laughed at me even though they were in church. Through her yellowed teeth, Duša whispered to me, It certainly was your family's at one time, but it is no longer. The only people with titles now are in the pockets of the Soviets and most of the Germans like your family went back to their rotten country, forgive me, after the war.

I felt both chastened and slightly out of control. I followed Alec and Duša like a baby duck until we sat down in another part of the church. And then something struck me. I leaned in to Duša and Alec: What did become of my family? I mean, Anneliese's?

Duša fretted for a moment, then whispered, Your mother and father, of course are no longer with us...time. Your brother Dieter, I am sorry, died in the war fighting for the wrong side, in my opinion, and God rest his soul, because otherwise he had been a very dear and respectful boy. Your sister Gisela, whom you adored, had married and gone to Switzerland just before the Munich Pact, and stayed and raised your daughter there. They are both alive, and they write to me every Christmas.

My eyes became wet as the lights came down. I said rather too loudly, I have a daughter! And then Alec's hand steered me aright as he murmured: *Anneliese* had a daughter. I wanted to know more, but the church went dark and the rattle of voices fell to only isolated coughing.

It was almost cruel that the first chamber piece would be the one Damek dedicated to his daughter Vlasta when she was born in 1929. The music started, a bright interchange of musical exclamations between the cello, two violins and piano, and I found I was crying silently but gladly. The music summoned memories I knew I once had but were long buried, suppressed by the transition from one life to the next. I could hear a joyous, inexhaustible child in the work, and I felt my womb as if I actually recalled carrying that child, knowing the pregnancy had not been difficult at all.

And then I found my other hand claimed by a strong, manly

one, not Alec's warm little hand or Duša's scratchy one. I didn't even need to look as I knew my former lover and husband was now sitting in what had been an empty space next to me. His lips touched my ear and he said, We had such joy creating her, do you remember?

I nodded.

Wouldn't you be happy with me in the house we created together? I've made sure that no one else can live there, only Duša. And then he emitted a low laugh and grazed my ear once again. I tried to pull away.

Why do you fight me?

I felt slightly sickened and his grip was hard and even cruel. I rose with a gasp, creating something of a stir among the intent crowd that had such regard for the music of Damek Svoboda, and I yanked myself from the grip, the pew, and the cathedral as the quartet continued without hesitation.

Rather than walking out into the April evening I had left only minutes before, I was startled to find brightness outside. I thought at once of the lights used for night construction on building sites, but realized it was natural light, sunlight, and I was no longer myself but Anneliese, in another suit dress of fine linen the color of celery.

(I certainly admired Anneliese's taste in clothing and wished I could have afforded the same.) I looked up to see a man passing before me and cried out: Uncle Leoš!

Ah, there you are, Anneliese, he said, I thought I had lost you. He was a stubby man in his sixties, beautifully dressed and smelling of *eau de cologne*. His moustache was impeccably trimmed while his chaotic white hair refused to be confined.

What did you think of the young man and his music? Anneliese (or I) asked.

You did not squander my time. Gifted. Expert playing.

It was *his* composition that he played, I said.

Yes, I know. Very capable.

I was a bit disappointed, but then he looked at me slyly. You know my dear, he said, I am close to retiring from teaching. I just want to finish *Příhody lišky Bystroušky* and compose. I am no longer young and my vitality comes in smaller drams.

Then who will sustain the legacy of Czech music if you retire?

There is Pavel Haas, whom I taught—Viktor Ullmann's work is quite accomplished—

Yes, I admire them too, I said in exasperation, but they do not quite say 'I am Czech' the way that this Damek Svoboda does.

A black robe floated between us as a priest offered his hand to Uncle Leoš. Mr. Janáĉek, said the priest, I am so honored to see you once again.

Uncle Leoš shook his hand with detached warmth. I watched as his eyes caught the young Damek staying close to the priest, nervously clasping his disarrayed music. You, young man, come here and don't be modest, said Uncle Leoš.

I was struck at how young Damek was, his suit too small and tight, his haircut uneven as if done at home by uncertain older hands. How moved he was! Throat wobbling, eyes flooded...

Sir, began Damek, I understand that you wanted to meet me. I cannot believe....the greatest of our composers...

Actually young man, you owe this young lady thanks. She has been coming to this church, I think not out of piety entirely, but also for the love of the music you create, said Uncle Leoš. I believe he saw Damek's reverence replaced at once with an instant infatuation for me, the young lady in question, and that's why Uncle Leoš smiled suddenly.

You, Miss, made this introduction for me? Damek stammered.

I just nodded, inhaling deeply. Janáĉek saw a feeling in me that could only have been a passion not suited to the Sabbath. He smiled again.

Let me take you both for coffee and cake, he said simply. I want to know more about your music, Mr.—

Svoboda. Damek Svoboda...

I felt an unexpected veil of wet on my face as the sunlight in memory changed into soft rain, and night. Before me were Alec and Duša staring at me as if I were a squid behind an aquarium glass. I was unhappy that my time with one of my musical gods had been so short, and relished my first meeting with Damek. I told my two collaborators about the meeting.

Janáček was a family friend and was terribly fond of Anneliese, Alec told me as we walked from the cathedral squeezed under Duša's vast umbrella. It was the older man's mentorship and love for Damek that transformed him from a talented organist with a handful of compositions into a composer of merit. Anneliese paid for his studies in the beginning, which was a sore spot for Damek once he found it out. It wasn't a mere infatuation that motivated her, Alec told us. Anneliese regretted having no artistic or musical talent of her own, and like many before her, decided to apply what resources she had toward someone with a true gift but limited means.

I spent the next few days listening to Damek's music, Alec and Duša pointing out a number of compositions dedicated first to 'a virtuous lady' and then openly to his wife. Duša and I also spent several hours amid her inebriating cakes and biscuits, with the crafty old woman telling me everything she knew about Damek and Anneliese. At one point Duša sniffed and looked at me with her huge, egg-shaped eyes, and whispered, You *really* could have done better than Damek; and then reacted to a violent flick of her ear by an unseen force.

Whatever Duša felt, the more I learned from these conversations, the more I listened to his shimmering and profane music, I was more infatuated with a man I had not known in my own lifetime. I shared his pride and anger at being a Czech in a country so long controlled by the Austro-Hungarians. I understood why he initially felt conflicted at falling in love with a woman of pure German blood who considered herself Czech. I practically recalled the binges in which he would disappear and then return to Anneliese contrite and self-loathing. I flinched almost in recognition when I learned of his long periods of enforced composition in which Anneliese only saw Damek long enough to announce that a child was coming, just to be dismissed angrily. I swallowed the pain of weeks of physical and emotional distance followed by Damek in tears begging for his wife's affection, sequestering them both in the bedroom for days. I could hear concert after concert of music by Damek's predecessors and peers whom he revered rather than scorned or envied; he saw them as allies in the same noble effort, to capture a remarkable people and country in the sounds of the orchestra and to make his statement lasting.

During this process I grew to like Alec very much, but I squirmed whenever I saw that he wanted to carry things between us further than what he called 'our project.' He often asked me what I planned to do when 'our project' was over. I said that I had someone to go home to in the States, though I didn't. I felt so badly when I saw how instantly he was deflated. My telling him how much I valued his friendship simply made it a more crushing loss for him.

Then one afternoon we were careless. I think we were worn out from days of talking about Damek and Anneliese, waiting for that moment at which I might turn things around with Damek and free us all. It felt like a summer afternoon though it was April, which also put us off guard. Duša was behind in cleaning, but refused to let Alec or me help. (I think she felt uneasy with the notion of me, Anneliese, cleaning!) Alec mentioned that he had had little sleep over the last few nights and would benefit from a short nap. We were within earshot of one another, but I saw I was alone and suddenly grateful for the solitude and even considered a nap myself.

I slept in a chaise for an hour or so, my head senseless, then awoke to hear people outside, down on the stone terrace. I found the voices irritating until I realized I recognized one, then a few. Without thinking to alert anyone, I went downstairs.

There was a table I had not seen before on the terrace and about twelve people around it, talking in low voices. Nothing seemed celebratory, and even the zither that someone strummed lacked brightness or energy. I was in a new dress, a summer dress, violet plain spun with folk designs embroidered at the hem, and I could feel a healthy cascade of my hair on my shoulders.

Well, I'm not leaving, one of the men said, and I knew that this was dear, dear Karel, Karel Čapek, sitting next to his brother Josef. The two of them together had written a startling play about robots that Damek and I had loved called *R.U.R.*; in fact, the word 'robot' had come from out of the play. I knew instantly that Damek and I loved both of the brothers but were worried about Karel's uncertain health.

Karel's brother Josef nodded. The Brothers Ĉapek will remain in Czechoslovakia, he declared, German occupation or not.

What difference does it make, really? a fashionable, bored woman said, leaning on a man I did not recognize. The Hapsburgs only left us twenty years ago. Germans here have always thought they owned the country, forced us to speak their language—

Someone muttered something more pointedly unpleasant about Germans, and a familiar man's voice reproached them: Please remember my wife is German. It was Damek speaking, at the head of the table.

Yes, I am one hundred percent German biologically, I said in perfect Czech, taking a glass of wine that I knew was mine. German was the first language I learned. I have only German relatives on either side for generations. But I was born in the Sudetenland. I live in Prague. My husband is Czech, my daughter is Czech, and I am Czech!

My friends cheered, and I looked across the table to see Damek smiling, a huge cigar between his flashing teeth. His face was red from the alcohol and the sun, and I'd never felt so much love coming from one person before. We stared at each other and I wanted so much to be right with him. Then I remembered our guests, and told them: And you, my friends, are the great writers and composers and artists of this stately, this precious land of ours. You have spoken out against the capitalists, and the dictators, the Fascists and suppression. And every one of you is marked.

Their voices rose in a slow murmur, reluctant, skeptical, and I shot back: There is someone, long a dear friend to me, who is in a place of authority to know all this. Yes, a German, and I am sorry to report also, he recently took a government post. He has confided in me that each one of you especially is endangered as you represent the true power of the Czech people. You, Pavel, being a Jew, and you too Viktor, you are both especially in danger...Get out of the country *now*.

A few started to object or dismiss me, but more were listening, thinking as I continued: Get out now before you're taken away. It's already happening in Germany. Don't give them what they want and what is most precious to you: *your lives.*

I saw them all listless or digging in their heels and I said very firmly: All of us can be in Italy in a day and a half, Switzerland in two. We don't even need to pack.

Someone made a remark about needing at least a few *koruny* to subsist, and I shot back: I can help you. You know I would not do otherwise.

They all faded from me, in the way my memories now came and went, and eerily I knew the fate of each one: Karel Ĉapek, spared the fate of a concentration camp by dying on Christmas Day, 1938; his brother Josef, dead at Bergen-Belsen, April 1945; and Viktor Ullmann and Pavel Haas, both dead at Auschwitz, October 1944. Only a sullen, stooped Damek Svoboda, composer of a jazz opera predicting the Nazi terror and demeaning Hitler, was left at the table, his cigar a mound of ashes on a saucer, and I knew his end also: death by suicide, August 1938.

Vlasta is with my sister, Dammy, I heard myself saying, but we were no more on the terrace on a summer day among friends for the last time. As if one dream was exchanged for another, I was walking into Damek's music room on the third floor where he was denying the world at a keyboard with music composition paper and pencils, cigars and Becherovka. I noticed myself in a blond tweed summer suit and a satchel in one hand, heavy enough for a trip of several days.

We have to leave as soon as possible, Dammy, I said firmly. I've packed your bag. I have the tickets. I've done everything to save your life, in short.

You mean, you and your lover have done everything? Damek snorted.

I was impatient with him. Gunther and I knew each other before we could talk—

This arrangement should make it all the more convenient for you to be with your 'childhood friend.' We don't need his help, and I am not leaving my country to the Germans.

Dammy, if I preferred Gunther, wouldn't I have walked out before? Why would I be here trying to pry you from that piano?

I've seen your letters to him.

Misinterpreting—

Telling him about your difficult husband. Unreachable. Telling him you loved him.

The way I love—

Why betray me in those letters to him?

Because I needed someone from home to confide in, I replied, and Gunther is one of my oldest friends. And then I realized: *This was our last argument.* The concern about the Germans. The lunch that preceded it, the sense of things ending unhappily. This was what I had to turn around, or I would be repeating it—as Laurel.

This realization nearly came too late as Damek was already backing me onto the open balcony three stories above the stone terrace. He spat a frustrated string of words, a contraction of all of his insecurities, the son of a prostitute, being Czech and not German, how he had taken my charity. Backing against the balustrade I could smell the cigar still on his breath and see my reflection in his opaque eyes, and I suddenly knew I was going to die here, helplessly.

And then I knew or remembered what Anneliese had done wrong: *she had confirmed everything he said.* Meaning to throw it back at him to show him the absurdity of it all, disgusted with his self-pity and perpetual anger, Anneliese repeated what he said to make him see its absurdity; but he was too agitated to hear the irony. Her response, meant to goad him into common sense, had been too much and he had pushed her to her death in anger and all by accident. So in what surely was my last moment of opportunity I tried a different track and grappled for the simplest, most healing response I could: I love you, Dammy, that is the only truth!

It was so brief and pure that it surely must seem feeble when I repeat it, but his face was overtaken by a look of bafflement. I could feel him ease. Anger seeped unexpectedly into his face again and I cried out, If you do this, we will never be together again. I will be sure of it.

Then anger fell away from him like a set of broken shackles. Damek looked past me to the terrace below in horror, gathered me up and brought me into the music room where he lay me on the day bed. What happened next was nothing I had foreseen; an act of lovemaking. I had no sense at all of time while we were in that room together and I had no concern about when I might come out of it. It was the most powerful connection I had ever had with another person, even if it was with the vestige of a person. At every moment I felt him as real: the hair and sweat on his surging back, his tongue, his thighs like marble, his commanding hands.

I learned later that Alec became concerned when I hadn't

emerged from the room after an hour, but Duša stopped him from disturbing us. Let them finish, my friend, she said to Alec. Let them finish their lifetimes.

Damek and I hardly spoke, but he told me that he would need to leave me, and he would find a way back. I would never be in danger again. And in half a breath, he was no longer there. There was an impression in the day bed, a slightly damp warmth, a scent even, that confirmed I had not been hallucinating. But the ghost of Damek Svoboda was gone.

I felt all kinds of things. Empty at this strange form of abandonment. Devastation that this man was no longer with me. But also, eerily, at peace with everything as I had not been at any time in my life. Everything was sharper to the eye and less dreamlike, as if a film on an aged picture had been lifted forever. I bathed, I found a fresh change of clothes. And downstairs I found both Alec and Duša waiting expectantly. I started to tell them what had happened, but stopped when I saw that they already knew.

You brought him peace at last, Duša said, pressing her hand to the air as if trying to feel a presence that was no longer there. She seemed changed herself. Whatever had tightened her face before, annoyance or bitterness, had lifted. There was a radiant lightness about her.

I could tell that while Alec had achieved a goal in freeing this spirit that had long eluded him, he also felt severe disappointment in what had happened. When he said, You've changed, Laurel, he meant that I was irrevocably in love with someone else. I felt sad for the little man, for I could never love him in half the way I loved someone who had come and gone in my life so strangely.

We knew 'our project' was done. We need to celebrate, Alec said almost tragically. Duša outdid herself with bright steaming bowls of *česnečka*, a garlic soup, followed by *řízek* or schnitzel and potato salad—and lots of beer. I can't tell you what I ate yesterday, but I certainly remember that meal. There was very little talk and both Alec and I went off on trails of thought, distracted, while Duša was the police matron bringing us back to the present. The next morning Alec asked me to record my experiences on tape, and of course I was selective. Another listless day, and it was time to regain my footing as Laurel Glessing, however much I loved Prague and cared for these two people. Alec too felt that he needed to move on, securing my permission to write about our experiences and quote me in a publication he would submit under pseudonym to avoid any backlash in the academy.

I remember leaving the house that had once been mine in another time altogether. Duša and I clung to each other like longtime friends and chatted aimlessly, agreeing to keep in contact through letters. We did just that until she died about twelve years later. Up to her final few weeks, Duša remained caretaker of the Svoboda house and I understand her visitors found her joyful rather than sullen as she often was prior to my visit.

Alec took me to the train station. He acted strangely, talking rather too loudly about trivialities, my suitcase, the lilacs he bought for me.

Your help has meant so much to me, Alec, I said in as caring a voice as I could.

My *help*, he said sarcastically. Yes, that's me, Alec MacAlexander: assistant to others in finding their way in life. I have that queer satisfaction and nothing more. He broke off and shuffled pathetically across the depot platform toward the street. I fought off a feeling of guilt and became immersed in something else, a magazine perhaps. It was not long after that I became aware of a calamity outside the train station. That is exactly the kind of thing I normally avoid, but I felt pressed to see what had happened—and discovered that Alec, in his distraction and self-pity, had walked in front of a moving car just outside the station and been thrown to the pavement. He had suffered a nasty gash to the head and his arms and hands were red-raw. Honestly, I was torn between being terribly upset as the cause of this accident to some degree, and being irritated at Alec for letting this happen. But when he was scooped into an ambulance I insisted in my compelling Czech that he was my friend and I needed to go with him.

An hour later and after much uneasiness, I learned that Alec had suffered, beside his cuts, only a concussion and a fracture in one arm, and would be all right. I insisted on missing my train to be sure that Alec made it back to the Svoboda Museum properly, and called Duša to alert her about the mishap. I am not surprised, Duša said flatly. He wants you. Don't let him manipulate you with this pretend accident. *You can do better.*

I savored that shot of humor on a broken chair in a hospital waiting room as impersonal as any I had ever visited. I was staring at the shadows of swaying trees on the uneven tile floor when I was visited by the feeling that Damek Svoboda was no longer gone. In the way that you can sense a change in temperature outside or a crowded gallery dwindling down to a few people—or the presence of someone you love come back to you—I felt a very strong confidence that Damek might have been set free, but he had also come back, and not at all to menace. I knew that he was in the room where I expected to find Alec sometime that afternoon.

Alec had previously explained to me the difference between possession and reincarnation during one of our preparatory sessions. I was not possessed by Anneliese but had lived her life before, whereas in some instances, a spirit can possess a person without entirely overtaking them. It's like having two drivers in one car, and sometimes one man is behind the wheel, and sometimes the other is, even if it is just one man's vehicle. So when I came into that room, Alec MacAlexander turned to meet my eyes, but it was Damek Svoboda who smiled and looked at me, and it was Damek Svoboda who told me that the accident had been no accident, but the chance for each of us—Damek, Alec and I—to find and have the lover we wanted, for years to come.

❧

Both of us were so astounded by Laurel's story that Mike and I could not look at each other. After several moments I put a hand on Laurel's, and Mike put a hand on mine. She held them both to her lips and kissed them, and then began to cry and laugh at the same time. It was everything for her to tell her story to someone who believed in matters of the spirit and would understand and accept her story as true. All that so many of us want is merely to be understood for our own peculiar truths. And when we are, I believe, we are never alone again on this planet.

We walked Laurel to her front door where she assured us that she would be all right. As she started to go into her darkened house, Mike said, Laurel...somehow I think that you and Damek will always be together. She stopped, and then offered Mike a look that was clearly grateful, but also downright chilling. Chilling because I realized she had already prepared herself to meet Damek again in this life, in whatever form he might inhabit.

Every sound in our house that night was magnified into the step of an unwelcome, transparent visitor. I only slept three hours and Mike just ninety minutes, and he came home from half a work day grumpy and terse, falling into a restless nap. Alec came home for a few days after that, and when we saw that pale, frightened version of him lifted onto a gurney and shuttled into the house, we knew he would not remain long. He died only a matter of days later, and without much hesitation, Laurel conceded to practicality and translated her life to an assisted living complex about fifteen minutes from where she and Alec, or she, Alec and Damek, had once lived. I went to visit her once, and stopped just outside her door. A low rumble of modern music seeped from her room, music which I knew as a string quartet by Bohuslav Martinů, one of Damek's contemporaries. Amid those challenging strains I could detect her irritated exchange with an unknown man—in Czech. I hesitated to knock on the door, and then decided to come back another time. I learned from a member of the staff there that Laurel had befriended a man who previously had shown no interest in much of anything, and they had become fast friends, as if they had always known each other. She died within a month of my only visit, and her new friend died not two days later; and Mike and I sometimes wonder aloud, when we are brave enough, where those inseparable souls, Laurel and Damek, might be today.

Acknowledgments

I am fortunate to have excellent friends who are also excellent critics. I am grateful to you for providing insights and suggestions on the writing of this novella:

Willie Considine
Alicia M. González
Esther Martin
Mike Pankratz
C Reed
Chris Schabow
Ken Sherman
Tudy Woolfe

Many thanks as well to my longtime and dear friend Karen Karbo for her tireless inspiration and encouragement.

Clyde Derrick's first novel *The Wash* won the Sol Books Fiction Prize for publication, while his experimental story "Each One As She Must" placed third in UCLA's "Considering Gertrude Stein" competition. His lauded short film Strider's House has aired on PBS and his plays Angel's Flight and Teshuvah have been produced on the Los Angeles stage by Write Act Repertory Company. Clyde earned his BA at Pomona College, where he won the Dole King Kinney Prize for writing, and an MFA in Cinema at USC. He lives in Claremont, California.

The Ghost Trio
by Clyde Derrick

Cover art by alamy.com

Interior typefaces: Garamond and Kepler Std.
Cover typefaces: Avenir and Copperplate

Cover design by Laura Joakimson
Interior design by Laura Joakimson

Printed in the United States
by Books International, Dulles, Virginia
Acid Free Archival Quality Recycled Paper

Publication of this book was made possible in part by gifts from
Katherine & John Gravendyk in honor of Hillary Gravendyk,
Francesca Bell, Mary Mackey, and The New Place Fund

Omnidawn Publishing
Oakland, California